A Magic Spark

Read more
Fairylight Friends!

Fairylight Friends

A Magic Spark

written by
Jessica Young

illustrated by
Marie Vanderbemden

ACORN™
SCHOLASTIC INC.

For Kate, who helped me find my magic —JY

For Lio, for all the love, laughs, encouragement, and coffee you bring me every day —MV

Text copyright © 2020 by Jessica Young

Illustrations copyright © 2020 by Marie Vanderbemden

Library of Congress Cataloging-in-Publication Data

Names: Young, Jessica (Jessica E.), author. | Vanderbemden, Marie, illustrator.
Title: A magic spark / Jessica Young ; illustrations by Marie Vanderbemden.
Description: First edition. | New York : Acorn/Scholastic Press, 2020. |
Series: Fairylight friends | Summary: Ruby, Iris, and Pip first met on their first day of fairy
school, and they immediately became best friends, testing their wings,
and enjoying their magical adventures—but sometimes it takes a little
time for a fairy to find her true magic spark.
Identifiers: LCCN 2019027460 | ISBN 9781338596526 (paperback) |
ISBN 9781338596533 (library binding)
Subjects: LCSH: Fairies—Juvenile fiction. | Fairies—Juvenile fiction. |
Magic—Juvenile fiction. | Best friends—Juvenile fiction. | CYAC:
Fairies—Fiction. | Magic—Fiction. | Best friends—Fiction. |
Friendship—Fiction.
Classification: LCC PZ7.Y8657 Mag 2020 | DDC 813.6 [E]—dc23
LC record available at https://lccn.loc.gov/2019027460

10 9 8 7 6 5 4 3 2 1   20 21 22 23 24

Printed in China   62
First edition, September 2020

Edited by Katie Carella
Book design by Maria Mercado

Table of Contents

The Magic Pool...........................1

The Cake 13

Star in a Jar............................ 25

The Seeds............................... 35

Surprise Party........................46

Map of Fairy Forest

Sunset
Meadow

Wishing
Bridge

Fairy Berry
Patch

Crystal Pool

Lily
Pond

Fairy School

Miss Goldwing's House

Moon Lake

Ruby's House

Iris's House

Pip's House

Meet the Fairylight Friends

The Magic Pool

Ruby, Iris, and Pip were fairy friends. They loved going to fairy school.

Ruby loved making art.

RUBY, BY RUBY

STILL LIFE WITH SPARKLES

Ta-da!

Iris loved flying fast.

Wheee!

BOING!

Pip loved growing things.

At school, the friends practiced their fairy moves.

They tiptoed.

TINK. TINK. TINK. TINK.

They flew.

ZIP! ZIP! ZIP!

One day, their teacher, Miss Goldwing, shared some exciting news.

We're going on a field trip!

Where?

You'll see.
Follow me!

The friends tiptoed across Wishing Bridge.

They flew through Fairy Forest.

They stopped beside
a sparkling pool.

Every fairy has a special
kind of magic.

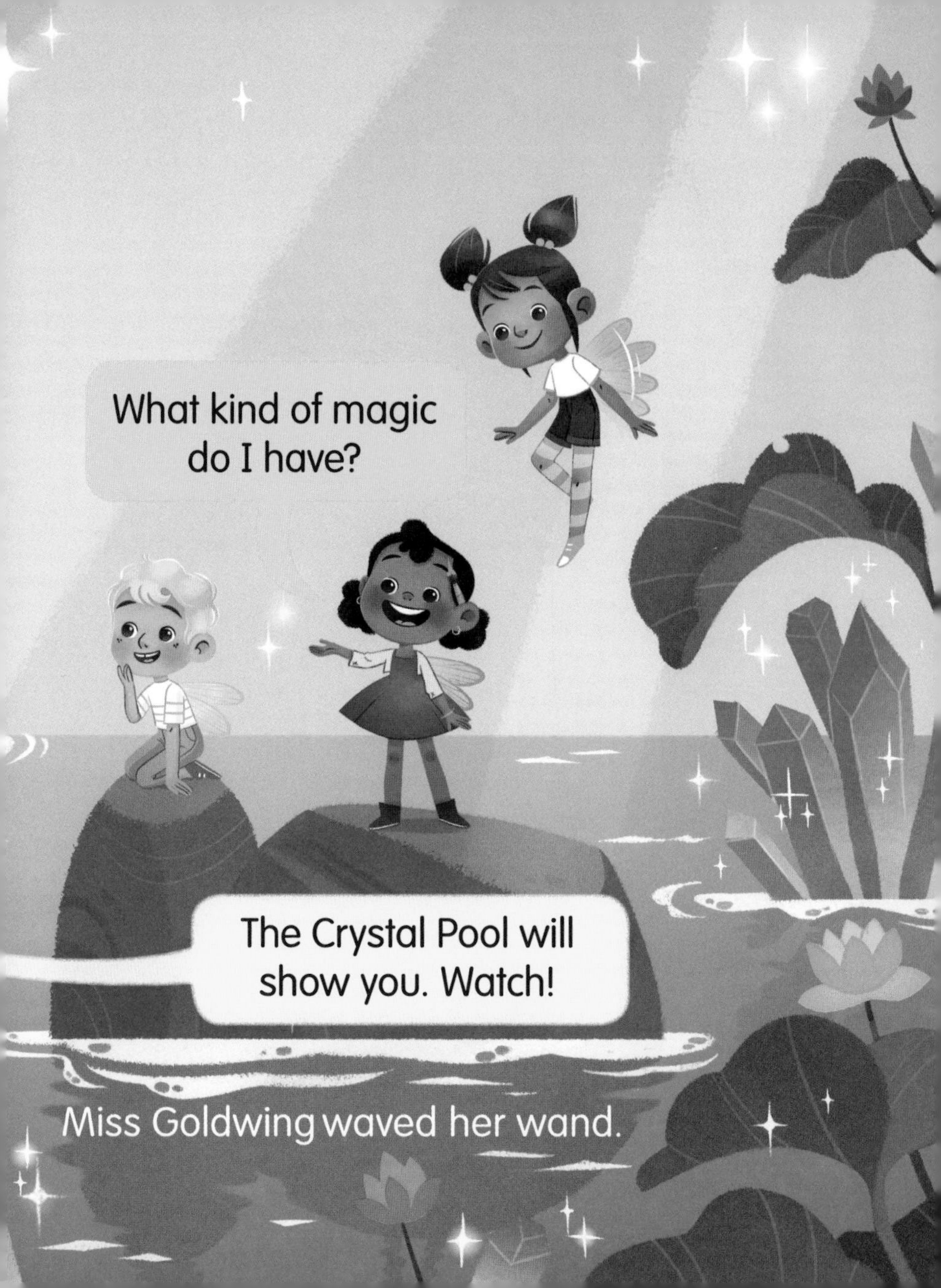

Miss Goldwing waved her wand.

BLUB-BLUB-BLUB. Ruby, Iris, and Pip each saw a different picture in the pool.

A rainbow!

A lightning bolt!

A flower!

The pictures are clues to your magic.
Where is our magic?
You'll find it when the time is right. It starts with a magic spark.

The Cake

Pip was flying by Ruby's house. He heard some loud noises.

CLANG!
BANG!
CRASH!

Ruby was in the kitchen.

Hi, Ruby!
What are you doing?

Hello, Pip!
I'm baking a cake.

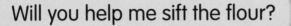

Will you help me sift the flour?

I'd love to.
But I have to watch
my flowers grow.

Ruby sifted the flour.

A while later, Pip came back.

Is the cake done?

Not yet. Will you help me crack the eggs?

That sounds fun. But I have to stretch my wings.

Ruby cracked the eggs.

CRACK! CRACK!

Pip came back again.

Is the cake done?

Not yet.

Will you help me
beat the batter?

YAWN!

It's time for my nap.
Besides, you're a
better batter beater.

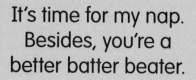

Ruby beat the batter and poured it into a pan.

She put the pan into the oven.

Soon the cake was baked. Ruby frosted it.

She showered it with sprinkles. There was a puff of pink fairy dust!

Sprinkle, sprinkle!

TWINKLE-
TWINKLE!

Suddenly, the cake was beautiful!

21

Yay! I found my magic!

Just then, Pip showed up.

Wow! That looks amazing!

I thought you were napping.

I'm all done!

Great! You're just in time.

Time to eat the cake?

No. Time to do the dishes.

YUM!

MMM!

24

Star in a Jar

Ruby, Iris, and Pip were looking at the stars.

Iris had an idea.

You should pack a snack. It might be a long trip.

Iris packed a snack.

You should put on your coat. It might get cold.

Iris put on her coat.

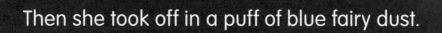

Then she took off in a puff of blue fairy dust.

I'll wave from the moon!
Vroom! Vroom!

Go, Iris, go!

ZOOOOO

She found
her magic!

28

OM!

Iris flew higher and higher.

She flew until she was too tired to fly.

Then she tumbled like a falling leaf.

She fell faster and faster.

Iris slipped off her coat.

The coat puffed up. Iris drifted down.

She spotted two friendly faces.

Yay, Iris!

You flew so fast!

Thanks! But the stars **are** too far.

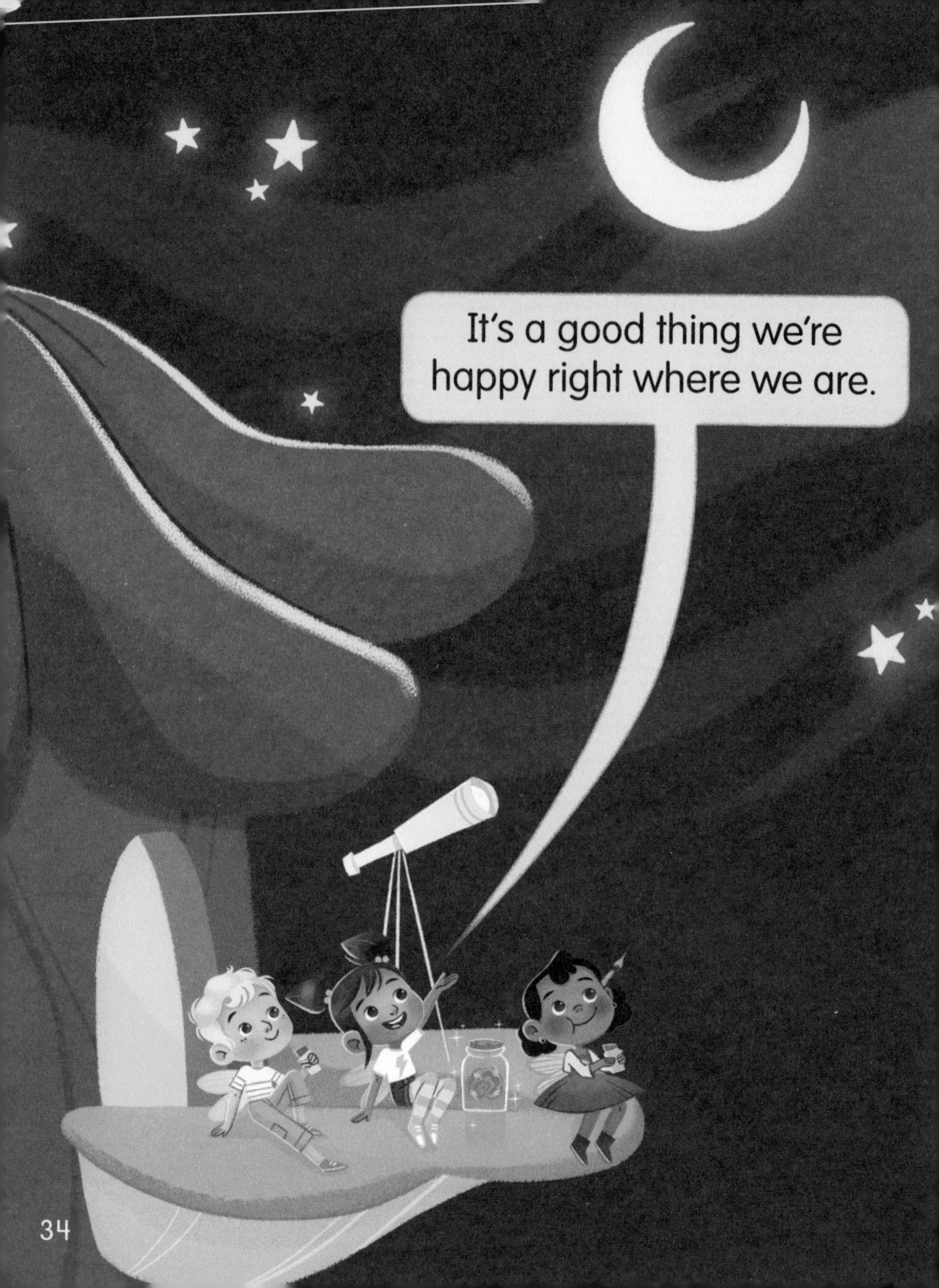
It's a good thing we're happy right where we are.

The Seeds

Iris was out for her morning fly. She flew to Pip's house.

Pip was in the garden.

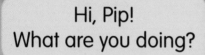

Hi, Pip!
What are you doing?

Hello, Iris!
I planted seeds.
Now I'm watching
my flowers grow.

I love their bright colors!

I love their sweet smell!

I love their soft petals!

Iris and Pip watched the soil.

Iris could not wait.

Grow! Grow! Grow!
Go! Go! Go!

Pip tried to help his flowers grow.

I guess I have the magic touch!

Surprise Party

Ruby, Iris, and Pip were picking berries.

FAiRY BERRY PATCH

We have so many berries.
We should share them!

Ruby thought of a fun plan.

Let's throw a party!

We can use our magic and surprise Miss Goldwing!

Pip did a flip.

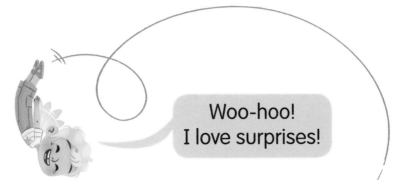

Woo-hoo! I love surprises!

Ruby, Iris, and Pip got ready for the party.

Ruby made things fancy.

Iris raced to find their forest friends.

Pip grew some flowers.

Just as the sun set, the friends spotted
Miss Goldwing.

About the Creators

JESSICA YOUNG grew up in Ontario, Canada. When she's not making up stories, she loves making art with kids. Her other books include the Haggis and Tank Unleashed early chapter book series, the Finley Flowers series, *Play This Book*, *Pet This Book*, *Spy Guy The Not-So-Secret Agent*, and *My Blue Is Happy*.

MARIE VANDERBEMDEN works from her barge moored in Belgium. Telling stories through drawing has always been her passion. Marie has worked mainly in the illustration of children's books and animated movies. Fairylight Friends is the first early reader series she has illustrated. When she is not sketching, she also enjoys photography, sculpture, and teaching ceramics.

YOU CAN DRAW RUBY!

1. Draw three shapes for Ruby's head and dress.

2. Add two ears, arms, and legs.

3. Draw Ruby's hair and shoes.

4. Draw one rainbow, one paintbrush, and two wings.

5. Add Ruby's face, earrings, knees, and jacket details.

6. Color in your drawing!

WHAT'S YOUR STORY?

Ruby, Iris, and Pip each have a special kind of magic.
If **you** were a fairy, what kind of magic would you have?
How would you find your magic spark? (Think about things
you love to do—or things you'd like to try!)
Write and draw your story!